AF256877

Pancakes with a Mistletoe on top

By Aurelia Foxx

PPRINT ISBN 978-1-7773188-9-5

To second chances.

Today was the day. I looked into the mirror and pinched my cheeks to get some color into them. I needed to look my best; it wasn't every day you met your best friend's fiancé. My mouth turned into a grimace at the thought. I quickly shook my head, dispelling the negativity but causing my brown curls to stick to my still wet lip stain in the process.

I let out some choice swear words as I picked my lipstick back up and then took my sweet ass time applying a few layers of touch up coats. My distraction didn't last long, and I was soon forced to face the music and push myself to leave my damn bathroom.

Before I knew it my boots, coat, hat, and mittens were on and I stepped over the threshold closing the door behind me. I turned on the car heater and waited for my windows to defrost. Putting my hand under my armpits, I watched my breath make little clouds of smoke. It was your typical winter day in Canada, everything covered in white stuff and cold enough to freeze hell over.

As the windows slowly defrosted, I let my mind wander and distract me from the cold. I thought about how I should act when I met her fiancé, what I should say to them both, if the guy was as much of a monster as I pictured him to be in my head. I obviously had some strong thoughts on my lifelong friend's current situation, but I didn't want to be an unsupportive bitch either.

The problem was that the balance of friend and unsupportive bitch was a very very fine one. I guessed it was all a matter of continuing to drop some hints about how I was really feeling, while I sprinkled stories with subtle morals or stories of people who took their relationships too far too fast. Of course, I would support her decision in the end, but I needed to know that I did all I could to inform her of how her decision could be the wrong one.

We were different she and I. I liked to over analyze every single decision in my life, and she trusted her heart with a reckless abandon, which I sometimes envied. It might give her some heartache later on, but she certainly spent less time fretting over decisions that might end up being wrong anyways. No matter how much you thought a decision through, there was still a chance that life took your carefully laid out plans and turned them on their heads. I still didn't know which of our methods was better, but at least our opposing approaches to decision-making were well suited for one another.

I took one more moment to rest my forehead on the steering wheel and let out some deep centering breaths before straightening up, giving the windshield a couple squirts of antifreeze and turning the key in the ignition. Here goes nothing.

***

As I pulled into the parking lot of the rundown family diner, I forced myself to relax my jaw and smooth the wrinkles in my forehead. As my hands begrudgingly turned off the ignition, my friend's voice fluttered in my mind as our conversation from a month earlier repeated once again in my thoughts.

"Oh you will absolutely love him Evie! He is just so charming, and nice, and really really hot. He really cares about me too. you'll see! Now I know you're going to call me crazy, but I just knew the second I saw him, like we were destined for each other or something, we just fit together you know?"

"I'm not sure I do know Stace, how long have you known this guy again? You only left for that internship 8 months ago."

"I met him a few weeks in, it's practically been a whole year! You have to trust me on this Evie, please agree to meet up with us. It would really really mean a lot to me ..."

I sniffled as the cold started to seep into the now turned off car. The neon sign proclaiming world best pancakes stared at me from the diner's front window, beckoning me to its heated interior and tempting me with one of my favorite foods. It damn well be the world's best pancakes because anything less was not going to make this supper any more enjoyable. I was also hoping they served alcohol with their all-day breakfast because I might be needing that too.

I opened the car door before my resolve failed and quickly ran to the restaurant's door. Someone needed to tell Jack Frost to calm down, I could feel my eyelashes freezing in the 20-foot distance from my car to the restaurant lobby.

As I pushed the door open, I plastered a bright smile on my face, as artificial as the fake mistletoe on top of the front door. God, I hated mistletoe. It had such a long history, with records of mistletoe being used all the way back to ancient Greece, yet these days it was only an excuse for people to grope you. Such a shame, yet another thing consumerism has f'd- up.

A quick glance around let me know no one else was here yet, I was opening my phone to check if Stacy had texted me when I was plowed into from behind. I looked up and the first thing my eye caught was the offensive mistletoe, before falling on a very tall and disheveled man. Immediately my hackles rose, this did nothing to help my bad mood.

"What do you think you're doing?!" I bit out at the exact same time the guy said

"So sorry! I didn't see you!"

We stared at each other in silence for a moment before I broke the tension.

"Ya, well please look where you're going next time" I said. When words failed me I tended to get defensive, and quite often it made me sound like a rightful bitch. I sighed and opened my mouth up to give a better apology.

"Will do Barbie."

"Barbie!?" My previous decision to apologize for my bad temper fell away. I wasn't sure what to make of that comment, if he was commenting on my plump figure, my heavily applied makeup or something else entirely. Whatever the reason, I damn well knew an insult when I heard one.

I looked at the guy more closely, if anything, he was a Ken doll. He had green eyes, a firm and square jaw, and an impressive build. His auburn hair had a red tint to it and, while disheveled, it still fell elegantly around his ears to frame his face. He had on a black and red plaid coat but I could still tell he was toned and muscular.

"Whatever you say Ken," I told him as I continued my perusal purposely skimming over his lower abdomen despite what looked like a security breach in the fly department. "Just leave this 'Barbie' alone because she doesn't need any more Kens in her life". I then lifted my eyes up to his and shrugged, as if to say, I've seen better.

Wannabe Ken was completely unfazed by my insult, he just smirked as he leaned against the hostess podium. His arms flexed in a delicious way. Man, he was definitely an asshat but he was gorgeous and he knew it.

"Someone's having a bad day."

Oh, that did it, today was not the right day to mess with me. A smile slowly crept up my lips and I probably looked a bit unhinged as I glanced back to his crotch area, this time fully taking it in. "Seems I'm not the only one, forget to button up and zip your jeans today? Or is that just something Kens don't have the mental capacity to know how to do?"

His eyes challenged me for a second before he gave in and looked down. He immediately cursed under his breath and turned around to do up his pants. He must have rushed here after a quick hookup and forgotten to button up his pants I mused. Typical Ken.

When he turned back the muscle in his jaw ticked, he looked me over, probably to find a flaw to comment on, but instead his jaw relaxed and his eyes fell to my cleavage and then up to my lips. His gaze got heated for a tiny second before he yanked his eyes up sharply.

When he caught me staring he just shrugged "I would make a comment but there really is nothing to comment on. Take that as you will."

Liar, I thought. He didn't like but, He totally liked what he saw. I wasn't sure why, but that gave me some kind of maniacal glee. It really really did.

I sat down on one of the chairs and crossed my long legs in front of me, then I took out my phone and tried to think of anything else but him. It was kind of hard though, I could swear I felt the asshat's presence near me and my mind kept oscillating between angry thoughts and very naughty thoughts. When I got this Stacy thing figured out, I desperately needed to get back onto the dating scene and get myself some action.

The thought surprised me for a moment, before a sense of calm rushed over me. I think I was finally ready. My heart thumped excitedly. Maybe this visceral reaction to Ken was my sign I was ready to move on from my last relationship, to finally let that shit fire go. My lips tilted into the slightest smile as I let myself both sink into that thought and the feelings Mr. Ken was making me feel.

Only a few minutes ticked by but it felt like it was hours. Keeping my eyes on the phone and not letting them flick to the man who now sat across from me felt almost like a winter Olympic sport. I didn't regret it though. It had been too long since I let myself indulge in these types of feelings. Who cared if it was for a jerk face like Ken, it was an exhilarating piece of progress.

When the front door opened with the chime of a bell and swirl of frigid air I looked up, grateful for the interruption. Any longer and I might have done something stupid. But when I saw my best friend, her arm hooked into the guy's arm, the light feeling quickly turned heavy and settled into a pool of dread in my stomach.

She swooped in slightly out of breath, her light brown hair streaked with red and green was swooped into a messy bun which somehow still looked elegant and put together. Witchcraft if you asked me. I spent only a few seconds on my friend's stick figure, perfectly applied makeup and legging and cardigan ensemble before I zoomed in on him. I could see what she saw in him, he was a bit different then her usual type but still had a sort of air of sophistication.

Carefully coiffed black hair falling slightly over one eye, defined cheekbones, and plump lips. He was in black jeans with a black jumper, the only accessory was a small silver piercing in his right ear and some kind of gold chain tucked under his shirt. He had no coat, but considering he was also out of breath I assumed they just took a run for it and left them in the car. Another sign that this guy was in fact her type, just as incredibly impulsive as her, always ready to have a laugh and try something new despite potential consequences.

As they stepped under the mistletoe Stace looked up and her mouth curved into a smile, she wrapped her arm around her guy's neck and pulled him in for a kiss. The guy looked stunned for a second, his back ramrod straight, before he relaxed and a big grin burst on his face as he returned the kiss with passion. I was all about expressing your sexuality but for some reason I felt myself blush at the sight. Despite what I thought about their decisions, I could tell Stace was completely smitten with him, and unless he was a good actor, I was pretty sure he returned the affection. Their kiss felt somehow incredibly intimate, like they were in their own little world and nothing else mattered.

A throat cleared behind me making me jump, I turned to throw daggers at the culprit, when I saw the sound came from none other than Mr. Ken those daggers became flaming projectiles. If he thought he was going to mess with Stace and her new boyfriend he had another thing coming. Didn't matter how I felt about the relationship, she was still my friend.

Matt pulled away from Stacy's now red and swollen lips

and looked towards Mr. Ken. As he caught Mr. Ken's eyes, his cheeks blushed bright red and he looked embarrassed.

"Sorry John. I didn't see you there mate." Matt said.

Stace pulled away from Matt who still had his hand around her waist and walked over to John with a big smile on her face.

"It's so nice to meet you!" she said going in for a big hug. John seemed absolutely uncomfortable with this development, his whole body language screamed that he wasn't as thrilled to meet Stacy as she was to meet him.

Despite my current feeling about Mr. Ken I eventually took pity on the poor guy trapped in one of Stacy's never ending hugs. Well, that and I was kind of annoyed at being completely looked over, so I took a page from John's book and cleared my throat loudly.

Three sets of eyes simultaneously turned to me.

"Oh my god Evie!" Stacy said as she changed targets and came barreling into me. She squeezed me hard as she continued to speak loudly and excitedly. "I was so worried you might not come! Matt told me John was definitely going to be here, and I mean you've never let me down before, but I know how you feel about all this, and I was worried…"

"Stace, breathe" I panted through her tight grip.

She let out a laugh and gave me one more tight squeeze before releasing me and backing up. "Ooops. I guess I'm excited."

A smile curved my lips, despite the fact I was still upset at this situation. Stacy had not only perfected the witchcraft of always looking polished, even in a messy bun, but also the witchcraft of always being able to make me smile even when no one else could.

"Well," Matt said, giving me a big smile and bringing us

back to the present. "I'm glad you could both be here. By the way, Evie, this is John" he said pointing to Mr. Ken "And John this is Evie."

John walked up to me, and I eyed him unsure of how he was going to play this. "Nice to meet you Evie," he said, extending his hand "Lovely name".

I arched an eyebrow and stared at his hand a moment before taking it. "Nice to meet you too Ken... oh sorry I mean John. Ken is this ass hole in the book I'm currently reading, how embarrassing." His large hand twitched a second in mine before he pulled it back and gave me a large smile. If I didn't know we kind of hated each other's guts right now, I would have almost bought it.

"Oh no worries, we all sometimes get fact and fiction mixed up."

Stacy gave me a look, which in girl language translates to, "Do you know him?" and "Is there something going on between you two?'. I shook my head and she smoothly turned the conversation around.

"Well, let's go get some seats shall we?" She led the way with Matt in tow and I fell back with John.

"So, Matt brought a wingman then. Guess he didn't feel like he could handle things on his own when facing one measly woman."

"No, he told me he thought it might be more pleasant if we had four people instead of three, something about not wanting anyone to feel like a third wheel. Obviously, I didn't fall for that bull crap, much like you shouldn't fall for the thought of Matt being scared of a woman. Whatever his reason was to invite both of us doesn't matter, invited or not

I would have come anyway."

"Why is that?" I asked taking the bait.

"Because I want them to get married as much as you do, which is not very much at all. I felt he needed someone here to help him see reason when he met his Fiancée's best friend."

"Who says I don't want them to get married?"

"Don't play games Eve. I'm sure my thoughts on the situation were as clearly written on my face as they were on yours."

"It's Evie." I corrected him with a glare. "And OK, I might not be happy with this either but there's not much we can do."

"If we work together, we can maybe get them to subtly see things our way, get them to postpone the marriage until they know each other better or something. And ya, I know it's Evie but I prefer Eve, Barbie girl."

Seething, I put my arm out to stop John while Matt and Stace kept walking towards the back of the restaurant, oblivious.

"I'm sorry John, but you don't get to change my name. It's Evie, not Eve, not Barbie, Evie. It's one extra letter, it's not that hard. As for your other plan," I let out a resigned sigh, "I'm down. But we both have to make sure that when we drop hints they aren't too obvious but also not so obscure that they don't get the message."

"Easy peasy. Stacy is our biggest problem. If we talk her down Matt will follow. Matt has a good head on his shoulders, he thinks things through. This kind of thing is just not like him. Stacy on the other hand, well, I just met your friend but from what I've pulled together this kind of impulsive behavior is not new to her."

I opened my mouth to reply, to say something to back up my friend, maybe something against Matt to even up the field, but I had nothing. John wasn't wrong, Stacy was super impulsive. I had assumed Matt was the same but this was apparently not in his normal realm of behavior, and it was kind of throwing me for a loop. The new information was cracking and shifting the narrative I had built about the situation.

John's lips pulled into a smirk, something I was beginning to understand was a signature move for him. "Come on Eve" he said as he walked off "We have work to do."

I watched his tight tush stroll away and cursed as I shook my head. Not only did I just let that bastard have the upper hand, but I also let his firm butt distract me, which only gave him more ammunition.

***

The waitress slid a large stack of chocolate pancakes in front of John and then a smaller stack of blueberry pancakes with a side of bacon my way.

"So," Matt said a bit nervously. "Now that we kind of got the introductions out of the way, how about some ice breakers?"

"I just love how organized you are sweetie!" Stacy said, giving him a peck on his cheek.

John leaned into me as Stacy helped Matt pull some things out from a bag on the floor, I hadn't even seen them bring it in, but then again, I had a lot of things on my mind.

"See what I mean? Matt, he's the type of guy to plan extensive ice breakers for a restaurant meal, not the type to get married after maybe 7 or 8 months of knowing someone."

"In Stacy's defense" I whispered back "she's never done this before either." In fact, most of her relationships burned up in flames by this time, but I conveniently left that part out. She hadn't had the best dating streak since her last serious boyfriend dumped her in the middle of a skydiving jump and then ghosted her. I'm still determined to find that jackass one day and give him a piece of my mind.

"So…" Stacy said as she lifted her head up from digging in the bag. Her cheeks were red and she looked a bit embarrassed. That was new, I could count on my hands the number of times she was embarrassed in public, and I had known her practically her whole life. Usually, she turned the moment around somehow, or strutted out of the situation like she did it on purpose. Maybe shy Matt was rubbing off on her as much as she was rubbing off on him.

"I might have brought the wrong bag. Matt had packed all these awesome activities and after our hot sex we were in such a rush that I must have grabbed the wrong bag. This one is full of books, books that we meant to donate. If Matt hadn't done what he did in bed I…"

Matt grabbed her hand and cut her off, his cheeks turning pink again. Poor guy, he'd better get used to Stacy or his cheeks would permanently look like they had were covered in red blush. "I'm sure they don't want those kinds of details babe… How about I pick a game we don't need supplies for, I wrote some down in my phone the other day in case."

Stacy showered him with praise while in the corner of my eye I saw John lean back in his seat and cross his arms. His large "I told you so" smirk was firmly directed at me.

Ass!

"How about we just do a good old game of truths?" John asked after a moment of Matt and Stacy scrolling through the list on Matt's phone. "If you back out of a question you are out, last one in the game wins and gets bragging perks."

"I'm game." I say even though I had never heard of a game called truths. I assumed this was John's way of setting up the floor for me and him to start our plan, operation "convince our friends to delay their hurried marriage without losing said friends".

"Me too!" Said Stace without hesitation. "I mean, unless Matt doesn't want to join?"

My brows rose, this was new too. Stace never cared before about what her other boyfriends thought about her choices. Sure, she listened if they asked for something but she never asked their thoughts before deciding to do something. Another small but drastic change. It seemed Matt was rubbing off on her as much as she was rubbing off on him, and for some reason, it seemed to be working in both of their favors. While she got him out of his shell and taught him to let loose and follow his heart no matter how impulsive, he seemed to be teaching her indirectly to be more aware of her surroundings and other people's feelings. I've known her practically my whole life and had yet to have that effect on her, despite the fact that those reserved characteristics were a big part of my own personality.

"Eve, you want to start it off?" John asked with a pointed look that confirmed his motive for this game.

My eyes narrowed at the nickname. "Sure thing Johnathan"

John returned my gaze, challenging me, before I broke eye contact and turned to look at Matt. If we kept this up, we would blow our cover before we even started.

"So Matt, tell us the story of how you first met Stacy and what your first impressions of her were."

Stacy rolled her eyes as she picked up her beer for a swig. Ok, maybe that first question wasn't so subtle, I'd work on it.

"Well, as you know, I met Stacy in London. I was also there on a work Visa and hadn't really made many friends, despite being there for a little while. The only friend I did have was this guy named Jerold. To be honest, I kind of hated the guy. He was nice enough, but he just got under my skin. So, Jerold drags me to this club he said is 'the' place to party. I… well I'm not a big party person, but again, at the time, Jerold was my only buddy out there and I didn't want to lose him by rejecting his invite to go out again. Anyways, I'm in the club and kind of off to the side just enjoying my drink when I spot this literal angel in front of me. No laughing man." He said with a pointed look at John, who then raises his hands in surrender.

"So, I try not to stare at this angel in front of me, but man, I just had this feeling I should go talk to her. So I manned up and walked up to her as she was dancing in the middle of the dance floor. The music was pounding so I tapped her on her shoulder to get her attention and Stacy here just sweeps me into whatever dance she was doing. Before I knew it, my body just kind of relaxed and I fell into step with her, which is weird. John can confirm I've never been a dancer."

"Two left feet is what he has," John says, taking a sip of his own drink.

"By the time we pulled away, somehow half an hour had

gone by. Stacy asked me for a drink. Jarold was stoned out of his mind by then and hanging with another group of friends, so I followed her to a bar a few streets down and things just kind of progressed from there. We started off with coffee, then went to Big Ben, a boat tour and some museums. Not sure when it happened, but eventually we both just knew and here we are." He finished as he gave Stacy's intertwined hand a soft squeeze.

"And all because of Jarold," Stacy laughed out. "Who knew a guy whose idea of fun was throwing Pop Rocks into the river Thames would be the reason I met the love of my life."

I filed the urge to ask about that story for later and focused on another piece of information. "Wait, you went to a museum with Matt?"

"Museums, plural." Matt said with a happy smile.

"Trust me Evie, I wasn't thrilled" Stacy quickly added "but for some reason museums in London are just better? I actually had a lot of fun."

"Maybe it was the company?" Matt said.

"Nah, that can be it." She teased right back.

"So," John says loudly, taking control of the conversation. "My turn. Stacy, why do you want to marry Matt? You know he has no money right now and no inheritance coming his way."

"Dude!" Matt said.

Seemed John needed a lesson in subtlety just as much as I did.

"No, It's OK" Stacy interjected "Matt's told me about your friendship John. Why you guys are so close and how you kind of see him as your little brother. I get that you're just trying to protect him."

I was obviously missing some key pieces of inside information but John neither denied or confirmed Stacy's statement.

"Alright, so Matt asked you to confirm some things with his answer and I'll ask Evie to do the same for me. I can be impulsive…"

"Very impulsive." I added

"Very impulsive" Stace confirmed with a cheeky smile my way "But I'm also smart. Maybe not in the textbook kind of way, but if life experiences could count as educational credits, then you could definitely say that I got a thorough education."

She looked at me to confirm and I nodded. My heart twisted as I thought about what she was indirectly speaking about.

"I wouldn't jump into marriage without being sure, I've learned better than that through my own… education. But with Matt, there's not only unexplainable things that makes this feel right, but there are also physical proof that what we have is right. Not only right, but as close to perfect as you can get. Matt makes me a better person. He kind of balances my crazy. It's more than that but words are Evie's thing, not mine. So, to answer your questions John, I'm marrying him not only for love, not only because I think he makes me better, but because I know it will work. I just know. We've been tested by quite a few adventures in London, and we only came out of them stronger. We had big fights, but always came back from them with a deeper understanding of one another. We're just good together. This is the guy I want to spend the rest of my life with. Why wait when I've never been so sure of anything in my life?"

There's a moment of silence after she finished where Matt and Stace just shared a look of such longing and trust that my heart ached. Then Matt gave Stacy a large cheeky grin and said "Ditto" effectively breaking the moment.

Stacy let out a loud laugh and pushed him back which only made Matt's grin widen.

"Alright, I'll go next" Matt said joyfully, "Evie, how did you meet your last boyfriend?"

I stiffened as Stacy's face blanched, all humor gone.

"You don't have to answer." Stacy quickly said.

I looked over to John and then back to Matt. I had made progress earlier tonight, an honest to God breakthrough. I wasn't going to let that experience get control over me again so soon. I couldn't let it happen. There was also no way in hell I was going down on my first question. If anyone was going down first it was going to be John. I could just imagine him gloating that I lost first and the thought set something in me aflame.

Matt exchanged a look with Stacy, "Ya, that was a stupid question. I'll ask another one."

"No. No, It's fine." I took a deep breath in through my nose and out through my mouth. "My last relationship was a little while ago. I met … I met him at a university post-grad function. He was a business major, determined to climb his way up and become a successful businessman. He was charming, too charming. Exactly the kind of guy who could charm you into buying an expensive knife set you really didn't need before you could even process what just happened. Before I knew it, I was under his spell, but… but he was never under mine. No one could break his hold on me, not even Stace, not even, not even him hitting me or yelling at me." I gulped and looked down as the tears threatened to spill. "The spell only broke when one night he took things too far… and I've been single ever since." I quickly finished.

Shit, I hadn't meant to share that much, but as soon as I started talking the words kept coming out, one after the other, tumbling out of my mouth until some of my darkest moments were revealed in front of two men who were basically strangers. It was both cathartic to let someone other than Stacy hear that story, and mortifying.

The oppressive silence that followed my story only deepened my shame. I started to sweat. I felt cold. My heart started to pound in my chest. I couldn't get enough air. I needed air. I had to get out, I had to get air, I had…

A fork swooped in front of me and scooped a piece of my blueberry pancakes.

I look up to see Johnathan stick the forkful into his mouth. As he chewed, his fork came right back to my plate to take another forkful.

"What the fuck? Those are my pancakes Jonathan!"

"Not anymore." John said as he shoved his next bite into his full mouth.

"You son of a bitch!" I said as I pulled my plate away from him.

"I'm not really a blueberry person but this is very good, really sweet. Mmmm! I think I'll take some more. Pass the plate over will ya."

"Like hell I will!"

John laughed as he made a grab for my plate. I realized then what he was doing. It hit me like a bulldozer. My heart released it's panicked hold on me and softened to become all warm and fuzzy. He was distracting me. He was distracting me, and it was working. It was working really well.

"Just take mine asshole." Matt laughed as he pushed his plate towards John.

"No way man." He said pushing the plate right back. "You got that weird ass carrot cake pancake thing. No one wants those."

Stace took John's side on how carrot cake pancakes shouldn't exist and how they were the Hawaiian pizza of specialty pancakes. Before I knew it, we are all laughing and exchanging lighthearted banter. When our game of truths started back up, I found myself enjoying it. My reservations for Stacy's marriage were slowly fading away as I warmed up to Matt and saw how much they cared for each other. Matt really was a good guy. I had a good bullshit meter, especially after my last relationship, and he didn't even register on the scale. Meanwhile, John was also growing on me. It seemed he wasn't as bad as I first thought, and I couldn't stop myself from being pulled into his stories, his laugh, his eyes, the little smirk he made when he thought he was right…

"My turn." John said, "Where did you get that girly gold necklace?"

Matt blushed even deeper than the last few times he was embarrassed. I don't think I'd ever seen someone's cheeks turn quite so red.

"Stacy got it for me," Matt confessed after some prodding from John. "about three months into our relationship. It was an important night. I mean, by the time she got it for me we were both kind of shit faced but it's still a night I will never forget and never want to forget."

"Oh. My. God. You kept it?!" Stace shrieked so loud the whole restaurant probably heard her.

"I always have it with me," Matt admitted. "But I only started wearing it recently. You're not always the most observant of those small thing's babe." he teased

"I guess anytime It would be in full view and not under your shirt I would be too occupied with other things ..." She leaned forward to whisper something in his ear when her arm caught on my cup of adult eggnog, spilling the liquid all over her shirt and pants.

"Crap!" Stacy cursed.

Matt jumped out of his chair. "Let me help you get that cleaned up babe, come on." He pulled her up from her chair and steered her towards the bathroom.

I quickly took a stack of napkins from the table dispenser and started to mop up the mess.

John walked over to an empty table and took another stack of napkins before coming back and helping me out.

"So, they're kind of great together, aren't they?" I asked him as we finished cleaning up the last of the mess.

John flicked his hair out his eyes as he put the last of the wet napkins into Stacy's empty plate.

"I hate to admit this, but they really are."

I watched him slump back into his chair and run his hand through his hair, my heart skipped a beat at the sight, and I inwardly chastised myself. Maybe John was growing on me, but we didn't start on the right foot and there was no way to know if his opinion of me had changed at all. I fiddled with my napkin to distract myself, my mind running over possible scenarios as he started speaking again.

"I don't really know what got to me, but I think I might be open to their marriage now, or at least as open as I can be after one dinner with them. It's still a little while away, at worst we can maybe team up again and do some kind of emergency intervention."

"Because that worked so well this time," I snorted. "But ya, I agree. I think if they are still the way they were tonight in a few months then they have my full blessing."

I looked up from my now destroyed napkin to see him eying me. "What?" I asked.

"That snort was kind of cute." He said softly, leaning in close. My eyes met his and I got lost for a second as they captivated me. I bit my lower lip as I imagined the feeling of his lips on mine, our tongues clashing as he wrapped his arm around my…

"We're back!" Stacy announced. "Matt got some paper towels from a waitress, and we got it almost all off… Am I missing something?"

John and I jolted back from one another, breaking the moment.

"Not at all!" John said, his usual smirk back in place.

A hurtful pang in my gut follows his words, had he been playing with me, did I imagine that sizzling tension?

We all went back to our food and our conversation picked up where it left off. As Matt showed off the gold necklace, I could swear John inched his chair just a little bit closer to mine, and it stayed that way for the rest of the meal.

***

"It was nice to meet you Evie, hopefully we can get together again soon. I know how much you mean to Stacy, and I would love to get to know you more."

"I'd like that Matt" I said truthfully.

"Good." He answered with a warm smile as he gave me a quick hug goodbye.

Stace gave me a quick side hug next. "Meet you at the car?"

I gave her a nod as she and Matt walked towards the front doors. Stacy had come in with Matt by taxi so John and I were stuck with taxiing them both back to their respective homes. Not that I minded, Stacy and I had a lot to talk about.

John and I stood there for a moment, neither of us saying anything but neither of us moving to leave either.

"Move two steps backwards." John said finally.

I eyed him curiously but did as he said.

"Now one step to the right"

"Why are you asking me to move John? Are you trying to get me to lead the way to the front door?"

"Trust me, Evie."

His words made me pause, before a victorious grin lit up my face.

"You just called me Evie." I said wagging my eyebrows

"And you just called me John," He replied without missing a beat. "Now take one step to the right."

I'm a bit thrown off by the fact that he was right, I had called him John, so I don't question him and just absentmindedly take a step to the right.

"Perfect," he said. He walked toward me, stopping with barely any space separating our chests and before I knew what was happening, he'd spun me backwards, his strong arms holding me a few feet off the ground. His hair seemed to glow from the light fixture positioned directly behind him. As he bent down, ever so slowly, my heart rate picked up. His lips hung a breaths distance above mine for one eternal second before his lips grazed mine in a soft but spine-tingling kiss. I leaned towards him, ready to deepen the kiss, to feel more of whatever this was, when he pulled back slightly.

"Mistletoe" he whispered against my lips before spinning me back into an upright position.

We stood there one moment longer, our eyes locked, as my breaths came in short spurts. I was still recovering from the attack kiss, trying to process what the hell just happened and how I felt about it, when he spoke again.

"Later Eve." Was all John said as he backed away towards the exit. "And don't forget your gloves." With one last pointed look at the ground beside my feet he sauntered off to the front door and then into the cold winter air.

I took a moment to compose myself before I looked down to my feet where one lone mitten was laying crumbled into a ball.

With one more deep breath to control my reeling mind I picked up the mitten and started heading for the exit. As I reached into my coat pocket to take out my second mitten my hand caught on a piece of paper.

Puzzled I pulled it out, the square piece of paper was not one I remembered putting into my pocket, but I did stuff everything and anything into my pockets. One of the reasons why my dryer sometimes rattled as it turned.

I quickly unfolded it, and just stared at what was a creased kid's menu, my confusion rose as I slowly turned it around. When I saw what was on the other side. I swear time froze.

"Hey there Eve, I don't know about you, but I think this meeting might have been our Jerold. This wasn't where either of us wanted to be tonight, and yes, it was Matt who brought me here, not a guy named Jerold, but I think this unexpected meeting between us has potential. Who knows? Maybe this meeting could lead us into something which is just as sweet as your blueberry pancakes. Call me? 710-210-1543"

With a skip in my step and the letter clutched in my hand I made my way back to my car. Me and Stacy had a lot to talk about on our ride home. We could start with how my hatred of mistletoe was really starting to change.

AURELIA FOXX

I hope you enjoyed this story! Be sure to leave a review online! It is always very appreciated and helps us authors in so many ways! More stories are always in the work so don't forget to sign up to my newsletter by going to my website www.aureliafoxx.com to not miss out on any details on upcoming releases or pre-order goodies!

* * *

About the Author

Aurelia Foxx is a Canadian Author of romance books. She likes to showcase the power of love and the magic of a story. Her romance books range from young adult and tamer, to spicy. You can expect a good amount of banter, swooning and humor thrown in to all her works.

When she is not writing you can find her spending time in nature, crafting, or thinking about one of her a million and one ideas.

www.ingramcontent.com/pod-product-compliance
Lightning Source LLC
Chambersburg PA
CBHW061105050726
47592CB00004B/1837